SHARE A STORY

The Tiger and the Jackal

Introduction

One of the best ways you can help
your children learn and learn to read
is to share books with them. Here's why:

• They get to know the **sounds**, **rhythms** and **words**
used in the way we write. This is different from how we
talk, so hearing stories helps children learn how to read.

• They think about the **feelings** of the characters
in the book. This helps them as they go about
their own lives with other people.

• They think about the **ideas** in the book. This helps
them to understand the world.

• Sharing books and listening to what your children
say about them shows your children that you care
about them, you care about what they think
and who they are.

Michael Rosen

Michael Rosen
Writer and Poet
Children's Laureate (2007-9)

For the children
of the Primary
Education Centre,
Swansea, V.F.

To Richie,
my big brother.
Big love, Ali.

First published 2001 by Walker Books Ltd
87 Vauxhall Walk, London SE11 5HJ

This edition published 2011

2 4 6 8 10 9 7 5 3 1

Text © 2001 Vivian French
Illustrations © 2001 Alison Bartlett
Concluding notes © CLPE 2011

This book has been typeset in Sassoon Sound City

Printed in China

British Library Cataloguing in Publication Data:
a catalogue record for this book is available from the British Library

ISBN 978-1-4063-3503-3

www.walker.co.uk

The Tiger and the Jackal

A traditional Indian tale

Retold by **Vivian French**

Illustrated by **Alison Bartlett**

WALKER BOOKS
AND SUBSIDIARIES
LONDON · BOSTON · SYDNEY · AUCKLAND

There was once a tiger
who was caught in a trap.
"Growl! Growl! Growl!"
said the tiger. "Let me out!"
A boy came running along the road.
Hop! Skip! Jump!

"Let me out," said the tiger,
"and I promise I won't eat you.
Please let me out!"

"Well," said the boy,
"if you promise ... then I will,"
and he opened the trap door.

"Growl! Growl! Growl!" said the tiger.
"Now I shall eat you for my dinner!"
And he pounced on the boy.
"That's not fair!" said the boy.
"You promised!"

"Ho ho!" laughed the tiger.
"But I'm a tiger, and tigers
don't keep promises!"
And he opened his mouth
wide wide WIDE.

"Moo! Moo! Moo!"
Just then, a cow came
trudging down the road.

"Cow!" said the boy. "I let the tiger out of the trap, and now he wants to eat me for his dinner. He promised that he wouldn't, so it's not fair, is it?" "Why not?" said the cow, and she trudged on.

"See?" said the tiger, and he smiled. "And now I shall eat you for my dinner!"

And he opened his mouth
wide wide WIDE.

Thump! Thump! Thump!
Down the road trundled
an elephant.

"Elephant!" said the boy. "I let the tiger out of the trap, and now he wants to eat me for his dinner. He promised that he wouldn't, so it's not fair, is it?"
"Why not?" said the elephant, and he trundled on.

"See?" said the tiger, and he
smiled even more. "And now
I shall eat you for my dinner!"
And he opened his mouth
wide wide WIDE.

Pitter patter! Pitter patter! Pitter patter!
Down the road pattered a jackal.
"Jackal!" said the boy. "I let the tiger
out of the trap, and now he wants to
eat me for his dinner. He promised
that he wouldn't, so it's not fair, is it?"

"What?" said the jackal, and he sat down.
"What did you let the tiger out of?"
"A trap," said the boy.

The jackal scratched his nose.
"I didn't quite hear you. Say it again."
The tiger's tail began to twitch.
"A trap!" said the boy.
The jackal rubbed his ears.
"Dear me. I'm not hearing
very well today. What did
you say?"

"A trap!" bellowed the tiger.
"I was in a TRAP!"

The jackal put his head on one side. "But I still don't understand," he said. "GROWL!" roared the tiger. "You foolish animal! Look! This is the trap!"

"Oh!" said the jackal.
"And where were you?"
"Here!" said the tiger, and
he jumped inside the trap.
"Look! Look! LOOK!"

"Aha!" said the jackal. "Now I see."
And he quickly shut the door.

"I think, Mr Tiger, we'll leave you
there a little longer, just until you
learn to keep your promises!"
And the jackal and the boy ran away
together up the road.
Hop! Skip! Jump! Pitter patter!
Pitter patter! Pitter patter!

Sharing Stories

Sharing stories together is a pleasurable way
to help children learn to read and enjoy books.
Reading stories aloud and encouraging
children to talk about the pictures and join in
with parts of the story they know well are
good ways to build their interest in books.
They will want to share their favourite books
again and again. This is an important part
of becoming a successful reader.

The Tiger and the Jackal is a traditional Indian tale about a little boy who very nearly ends up being dinner for a hungry tiger. The jackal helps him to escape danger but what upsets the boy most is that the tiger didn't keep his promise. Here are some ways you can share this book:

• The traditional telling of the story helps you read it aloud in an interesting and lively way. This helps children to understand, enjoy and remember it.

• As you re-read the story, children gradually remember it and join in with the repeated phrases. This builds the confidence of young readers.

• Talking together about the story during reading and afterwards helps children to make sense of what they hear and read.

• Children's questions can take conversations about the story in interesting and valuable directions. It's a good way to develop their understandings about the book and the world they live in.

• Drawing either a picture or mask of one of the characters is a good prompt to help them tell the story in their own words. For example, they could wear a tiger mask and tell his side of the story.

SHARE A STORY
A First Reading Programme
From Pre-school to School

Beginnings – 2 years+

Look Out, Suzy Goose — Petr Horáček

Walking Through the Jungle — Julie Lacome — Introduced by Michael Rosen

Hello, Goodbye — David Lloyd, Louise Voce — Introduced by Michael Rosen

Ten in the Bed — Penny Dale — Introduced by Michael Rosen

This Is the Bear — Sarah Hayes, Helen Craig — Introduced by Michael Rosen

The Big Wide-Mouthed Frog — Ana Martín Larrañaga — Introduced by Michael Rosen

Early Steps – 3 years+

A New House for Mouse — Petr Horáček — Introduced by Michael Rosen

The Train Ride — June Crebbin, Stephen Lambert — Introduced by Michael Rosen

The Other Day I Met a Bear — Russell Ayto — Introduced by Michael Rosen

Old MacDonald Had a Farm — Jane Chapman — Introduced by Michael Rosen

The Tiger and the Jackal — Vivian French, Alison Bartlett — Introduced by Michael Rosen

Zed's Bread — Mick Manning, Brita Granström — Introduced by Michael Rosen

Next Steps – 4 years+

The Hairy Toe — Daniel Postgate — Introduced by Michael Rosen

The True Story of Humpty Dumpty — Sarah Hayes, Charlotte Voake — Introduced by Michael Rosen

Beans on Toast — Paul Dowling — Introduced by Michael Rosen

Over in the Meadow — A Counting Rhyme — Louise Voce — Introduced by Michael Rosen

Polly Dunbar Dog Blue — Introduced by Michael Rosen

Night-night, Knight And Other Poems — Michael Rosen, Sue Heap — Introduced by Michael Rosen

Taking Off – 5 years+

"Have You Seen the Crocodile?" — Colin West — Introduced by Michael Rosen

Handa's Surprise — Eileen Browne — Introduced by Michael Rosen

The Ravenous Beast — Niamh Sharkey — Introduced by Michael Rosen

One, Two, Flea! — Allan Ahlberg, Colin McNaughton — Introduced by Michael Rosen

Dinosaurs' Day Out — Nick Sharratt — Introduced by Michael Rosen

The Old Woman and the Red Pumpkin — Betsy Bang, Rachel Merriman — Introduced by Michael Rosen

Sharing the best books makes the best readers

WALKER BOOKS

www.walker.co.uk